MY MUM HAS X-RAY VISION

EE

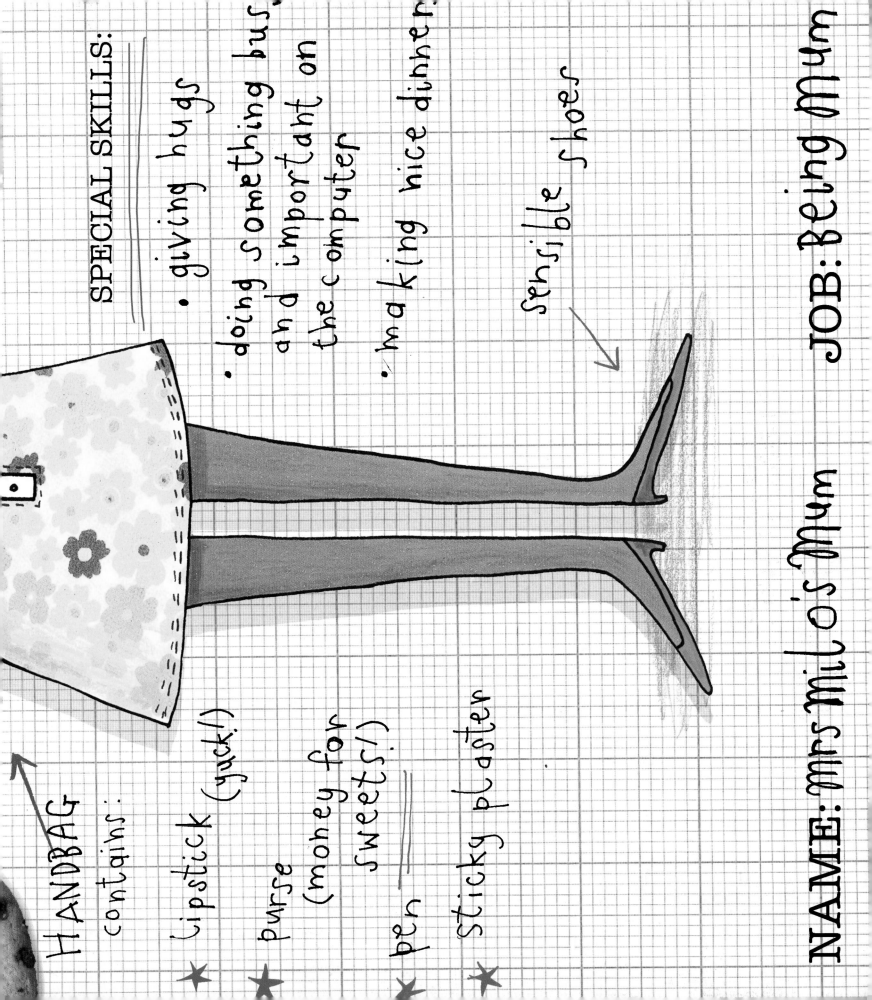

SPECIAL SKILLS:

- giving hugs
- doing something busy and important on the computer
- making nice dinner

sensible shoes

HANDBAG
contains:

★ lipstick (yuck!)
★ purse (money for sweets!)
★ pen
★ sticky plaster

NAME: Mrs Milo's Mum

JOB: Being Mum

For my Supermum!
AM

For the House of Handley:
Jill, Brian and Jennifer
(and of course Ben and Bert the cats!)
ATS

First published in 2010
by Scholastic Children's Books
Euston House, 24 Eversholt Street
London NW1 1DB
a division of Scholastic Ltd
www.scholastic.co.uk
London ~ New York ~ Toronto ~ Sydney ~ Auckland ~
Mexico City ~ New Delhi ~ Hong Kong

Text copyright © 2010 Angela McAllister
Illustrations copyright © 2010 Alex T. Smith

HB ISBN 978 1407 10537 6
PB ISBN 978 1407 10538 3

The moral rights of Angela McAllister and Alex T. Smith have been asserted.
Papers used by Scholastic Children's Books are made from wood
grown in sustainable forests.

MY MUM HAS X-RAY VISION

THE GOSSIP

■ SCHOLASTIC

MILO'S MUM was like all the other mums. She had ordinary hair, ordinary clothes and a nice smile.

MILO'S MUM
was just like all
the other mums…

EXCEPT she could see through things. Milo was pretty sure she had

X-RAY VISION.

On Monday, he was wrestling with a **GIANT SEa MONSTER** when **MUM** shouted from downstairs.

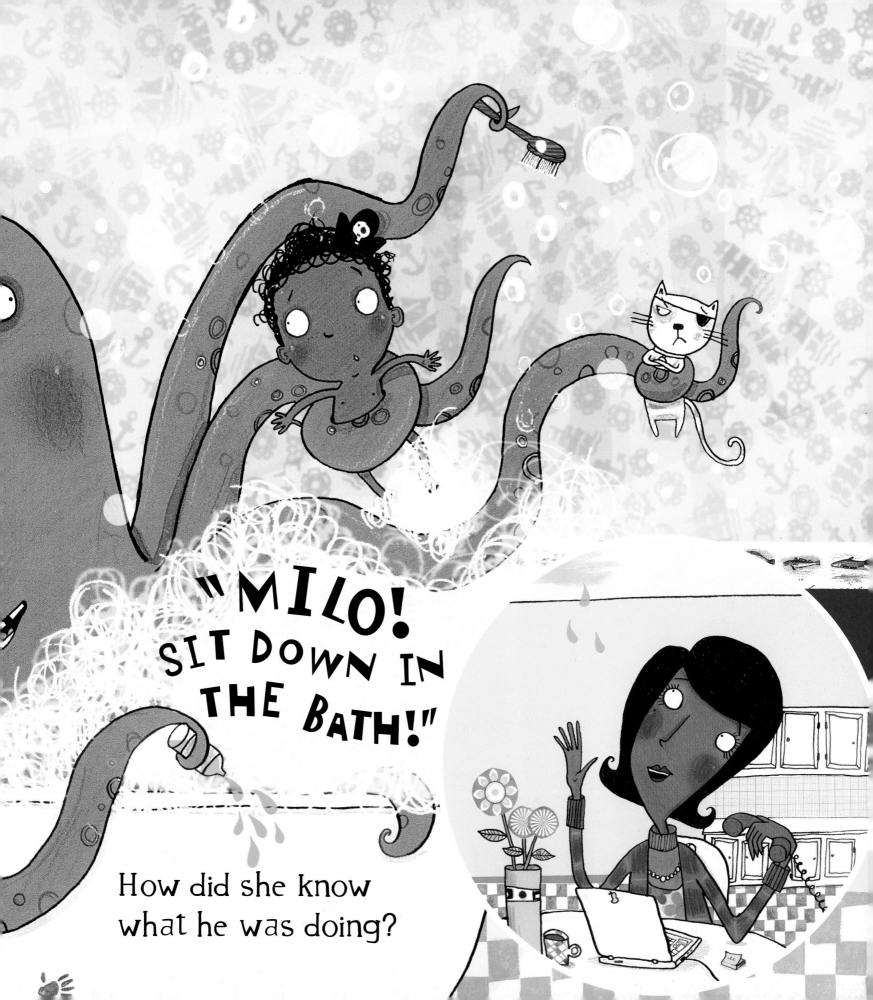

"MILO! SIT DOWN IN THE BATH!"

How did she know what he was doing?

On Wednesday, he was brewing up spells in a mountain cave to defeat a **POWERFUL WIZARD** when **MUM** yelled from the kitchen.

"**MILO!** DON'T USE MY **SAUCEPANS** IN THE **GARDEN!**"

How did she know
that he had them?

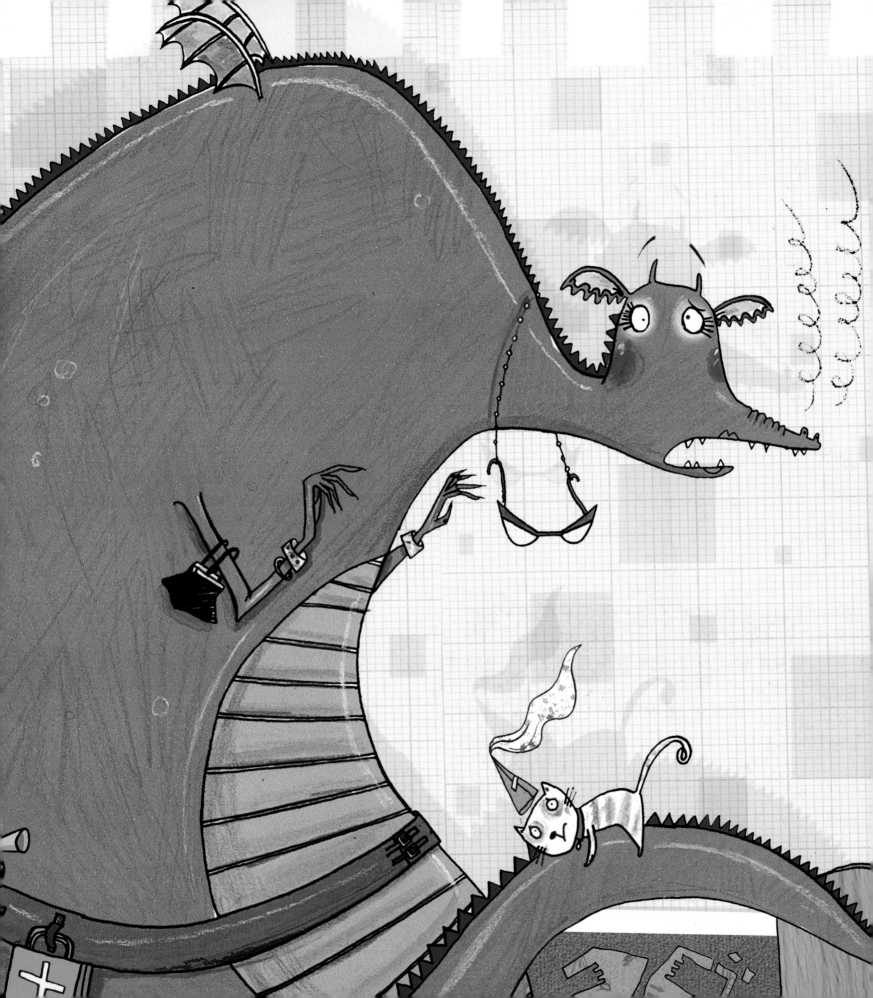

On Friday, he was defending his castle from an **ENORMOUS FIRE-BREATHING DRAGON**, when **MUM** called up from the sitting room.

"MILO! DON'T BOUNCE ON THE BED!"

How did she know where he was?

Thump!

"It's really weird," Milo said to his friend Lola. "My **MUM** can see what I'm doing when she isn't there. She must have **X-RAY VISION**."

"I'll ask my brother," said Lola. "He's always reading **SUPERHERO** comics. He'll know about **X-RAY VISION**."

But Milo had to find out for himself.
"I'll give **MUM** a test," he thought.

On Saturday, when **MUM** asked him
to help bring in the shopping, Milo
crept upstairs and hid
in the wardrobe.

"MILO!" called
MUM. "WHERE ARE
YOU GOING?"

Milo smiled to himself.

"If **MUM** comes right inside, right up the stairs, right into the bedroom, and opens the wardrobe door, then I'll know for sure that she has **X-RAY VISION**."

Milo waited.
But **MUM** didn't come.

Aargh!

Milo waited.
Still **MUM** didn't come.
Maybe she couldn't see
through wardrobes...

Still Milo waited.
Maybe **MUM** couldn't
see through doors...

"Maybe **MUM** has forgotten me," thought Milo.

Then suddenly he heard footsteps. Someone came up the stairs. Someone opened the door.

"MUM!" called Milo and out he jumped.

But it wasn't **MUM**.

Lola offered Milo a gumdrop. "My brother says
that mums never have **X-RAY VISION**," she said.
"And he knows."

"He's right," sighed Milo. "I was wrong.
I hid but she couldn't find me.
She's **NOT** a **SUPERHERO**.
She's just an ordinary **MUM**, like all the rest."

Then they heard a
rustle in the hall.

"LET'S PUT THIS SHOPPING AWAY," said MUM.

So Milo and Lola helped MUM, and she thanked them with her nice, ordinary smile.

"Come on, Lola," said Milo,
"let's make a den now."
But just as they made a dash
for the door...
"MILO!" shouted **MUM**.
**"DON'T HIDE THAT PACKET
OF CRISPS UP YOUR JUMPER!"**

Milo looked at **MUM** suspiciously. Then
a big grin crept onto his face.
"Guess what?" he whispered to Lola.

"I think my **MUM** has **EYES** IN THE **BACK OF HER HEAD!**"

NAME: SUPERMUM JOB: Saving the world!

rocket boots

DRAMATIC RESCUE: Supermum rescues her n
Mrs Ethel Hogsbottom who fell from her bedr

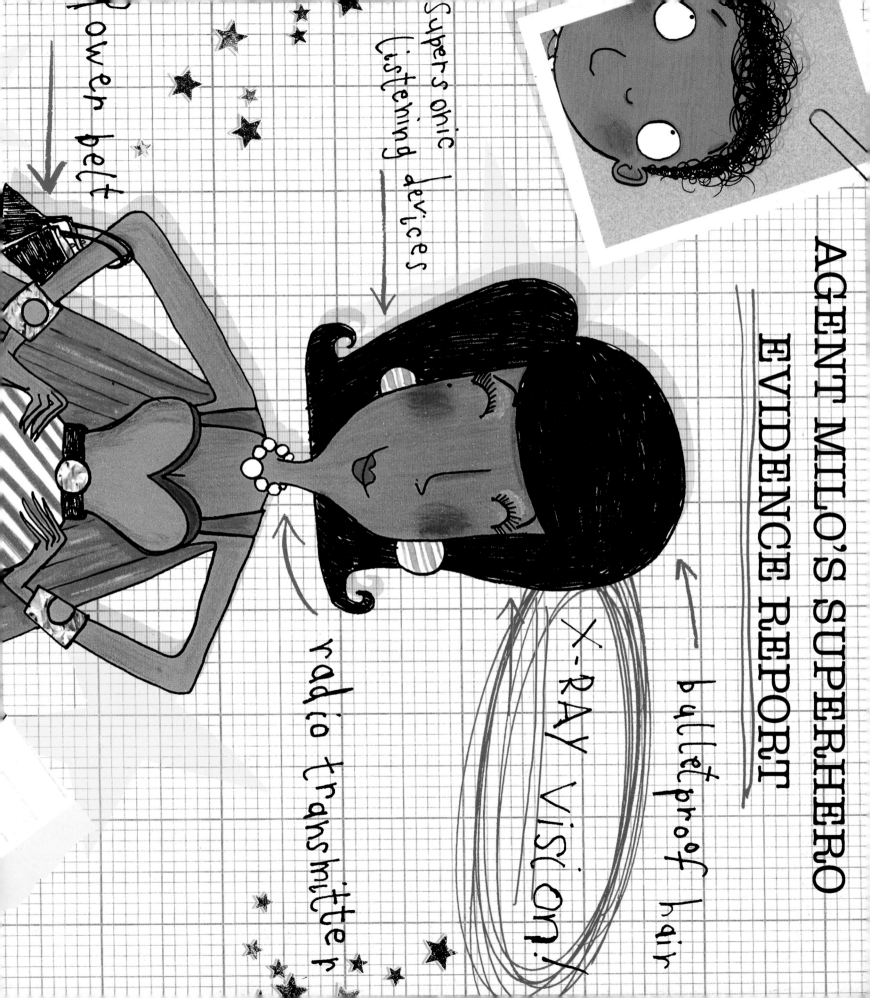

THE END